I DIDN'T ASK FOR THIS

Evangelist Barbara Hawthorne

Copyright © 2024 All

Rights Reserved

ISBN:

978-1-964365-33-6

About The Author

Evangelist Barbara Hawthorne is a native Memphian, a motivational teacher, speaker, community outreach and intercessor called, appointed and anointed by God. She has served in many offices of God under serval ministries locally and internationally. (Ephesian 4:12) she is equipped to serve the people of God so that, the body of Christ may be built up, NIV. She is woman that loves God and the people of God. Tested my life experiences in her health, employment, and family tragedies. Never gave up on God when the trials of life affected her faith, and she believed in God for the results. She stands firm totally depending on Him in her teaching, in her prayers, speaking, and ministering with the simplicity of the Holy Spirit. Her gift of teaching prayer is a gift needed in this season "for such a time as this." Her love for prayer was a mantle passed down from her grandparents. *"My grandfather was a man of prayer and taught Sunday school, and my grandmother was an usher and prayer warrior. The first most important prayer prayed to God was for my mother. Single mother and her grandparents raised her."* Barbara stated.

She is an educator who has earned several degrees. This allowed her the opportunity to prepare her for the path of ministry. She pursued her education as she earned her BA in Biblical studies from Jacksonville Theology. She studied additional biblical classes and Business from Crichton College and received an undergrad degree in BS/ Business. Studying at Mason Temple's biblical classes and receiving a certificate through the FGBCF education division to teach throughout the region while serving as the International Elder central region, receiving a counseling certificate through Healing Center /accredited through Methodist Hospital and Master MBA Public Administration from Strayer University.

She has done community outreach and recorded with Billy Rivers and the Angelic Voices of Faith on two live recordings. She has marched along with great leaders in great movements. She also worked as a volunteer worker with the Juvenile Court as a CASA worker, standing for Court Appointed Advocacy for at-risk kids. She has worked with several ministries in ministering to incarcerated women, juveniles and men. She served on several non-profits as a board member, such as Beyarata Mobile Disaster Tax Services, My Big Brother Keeper, Faithful Few, CHAMPS etc.

She earned an Honorary Doctor of Ministry from ICM, a Master of Theology from Liberty University, and a Chaplain CPE Certification from ACPE. Special thanks to Pastor John and Pastor Leslie Sielbing of Life Church Memphis, as well as Pastor Paul and Co-Pastor Debra Reed of Newfriendship Memphis, TN.

Dedication

In memory of my two great nephews, William T. Rose and Barron R. Thomas II, whose lives were cut short too soon. William, a victim of wrongful death in 2020, and Barron, lost to the complications of diabetes in the same year. 'I Didn't Ask for This' will serve as a healing tool, impacting lives through brief prayers and scriptures. Through my unwavering love, I hope to demonstrate the power of prayer and the belief in God for the ultimate outcome.

Special Thanks

A special thank you to these pastors, ministers, and artists for their songs and lyrics: I thank my God in all my remembrance of you, always in every prayer of mine for you all, making my prayer with joy.

Lady Gaga, Mary J. Blige, Justin Bieber, Jennifer Hudson, Fantasia Barrino, Milton Brunson - in memory, Carrie Underwood, Kelley Clarkson, Helen Baylor, Williamson Christian Mas Choir, Sarah McLaurin, Yolanda Adams, Donnie McClurkin, Tenors, Celine Dion, Andrea Bocelli, and Vanessa Bell.

Special Thanks to my Pastor John Siebling and the Life church family of Memphis, TN, God's gift that changes everything. Ephesians 2: 8-9 ESV For by grace you have been saved through faith. In addition, this is not your own doing; it is the gift of God, [9]not a result of works, so that no one may boast.

Acknowledgments

I like to give special thanks to each artist and the Word of God to help encourage the victims, families, parents, and friends. To encourage them to educate themselves and break the cycle and silence that is weighing them by collaborating healing through this book, the lyrics, and biblical phrases.

I was able to share the real-life incidents from just praying with these people; some went on to receive more medical help through domestic violence center, children were referred to child advocates, and some now have private therapists they work with as well. However, there is still insufficient for people, children, and women to strive and seek. To read this book is a release of hope for the future.

I thank God for the gift of prayer, speaking, and teaching his word to help people. I thank God for the opportunity to help believers and non-believers that there is hope in every area of abuse. I do not take credit for my gift of prayer being from God, the mantle of my mother , grandparents, family members and when I pray I can feel Gods heart releasing healing in atmosphere through the spirit of God. I am grateful to senior Pastor John Siebling of Life Church of Memphis, TN for his teaching and practical principle through the word of God and a church family of diversity, innovation in teaching, and the outstanding outreach branches from the tree of life throughout Memphis.

I thank God for the spiritual men and women in my life. Special recognition to women of wisdom and the gifting of prayer: Mother Katherine Clay, Prophetess Gladness Fulton,

Beverly S. Clark, Pastor Terry Marr, Mother Lille Thurman, Wiley Henry and many, many more, along with International level FGBCF.

Foreword

By Wiley Henry

Life can be mundane and complicated sometimes. But when you add to the mix physical, emotional and sexual abuse – which is often perpetrated by loved ones, a trusted friend, or even the clergy – this trichotomy can become explosive and lead to a wretched lifestyle or worse.

But there is hope, help, and healing for those whose lives have been upended or shattered by such traumatic experiences. Prayer. It's the answer when lives are torn apart; when grief is quadrupled with grief; when anguish rips a hole in the soul; and when life no longer matters and lay waste when one gives up the fight.

In the following chapters of this book, "I Didn't Ask for This," the author, Evangelist Barbara Ann Hawthorne, looks at this scourge in our society through the lens of her Christian faith, Bible study, intercessory prayer, and from the perspective of someone like a counselor who can provide much-needed professional help. Each, however, is germane to one's healing, mental stability, and restoration. But it all depends on the victim(s) and their willingness to turn their lives completely over to Him – the God of Abraham, Isaac and Jacob, and, of course, the same God of today's Christians – who, in fact, is omnipotent and has all the answers.

Prayer is – and has been – the foundation of Evangelist Hawthorne's life and spiritual journey. In fact, it was through the writings and stories inscribed in her prayer journal that sparked the writing of "I Didn't Ask for This." She'd witnessed damaged souls and lives engulfed with pain and emotional distress that prompted her to do something that would inform and shed light on the darkness that pervades mankind.

There is no harm in crying out for help, Evangelist Hawthorne said. But cry, nonetheless, knowing that problems are solvable, and solutions are within one's grasp in a biblical sense. "I Didn't Ask for This," in terms of biblical sense, is replete with scriptures that support the author's argument that one can heal from such a gaping wound that can fester if left unattended. In essence, carefully chosen scriptures in this book are the building blocks of healing, which builds up and strengthens the mind, body and soul.

"I Didn't Ask for This" is more than a journal experience for readers. It's Evangelist Barbara Ann Hawthorne's attempt to bring attention to physical, emotional and sexual abuse at the hands of those who prey on the weak and unsuspected – even in the church, a place supposedly of refuge and safety, where voices often remain silent.

Contents

Introduction

"I Didn't Ask For This" is a book that expresses the story of a song that was recorded by an artist, Lady GaGa and co-written by Dianne Warren: "Until This Happen To You" with lyrics: *You tell me it gets better, it gets better in time. You say I'll pull myself together, pull it together. You'll be fine. Tell me what the hell do you know. What do you know. Tell me how the hell could you know. How could you know. 'Til it happens to you, you don't know. How it feels.* Lady Gaga performed this at the Oscars 2016 on live television. It was so demonstrative in ways expressive with the emotions of rape that had happen on college campus sexual, domestic violence, child abuse, and physical abuse placing them all together that was powerful design of all forms of abuse. I know you see the word, hell, stay with me. The word represents darkness, the rape, the abuse, and the silence pain.

Psalms 23:4

[4]Yea, though I walk through the valley of the shadow of death, I will fear no evil: for thou art with thy rod; thy staff and me, they comfort me.

Genesis 2: 18-25 - New International Versions (NIV)

[18] The Lord God said, "It is not good for the man to be alone. I will make a helper suitable for him."

[19] Now, the Lord God had formed out of the ground all the wild animals and all the birds in the sky. He brought him or her to the man to see what he would name him or her; and

whatever the man called each living creature, that was its name. [20] So, the man gave names to all the livestock, the birds in the sky and all the wild animals.

But for Adam, no suitable helper was found. [21] So the Lord God caused the man to fall into a deep sleep; and while he was sleeping, he took one of the man's ribs[b] and then closed up the place with flesh. [22] Then the Lord God made a woman from the rib[c] he had taken out of the man, and he brought her to the man. [23] The man said, "This is now bone of my bones and flesh of my flesh; she shall be called 'woman,' for she was taken out of man." [24] That is why a man leaves his father and mother and is united to his wife, and they become one flesh.

[25] Adam and his wife were both naked, and they felt no shame.

When God created woman from the rib of Adam, representing the mystical unity of the couple's heart and their lives, God has always intended for women, girls, and humankind to be safe and respected. This was not voided because of college students of a prestige university campus, or young small kid's boys or girls, 25 plus women looking for the courage to break the silence, to break the cycle of generation curses of violation.

While in prayer for a few days and having a visit of the presence of God and the Holy Spirit. God began to bring back memories and prayers in my journals of various prayers and scenarios that I had shared with people for damaged emotions. I prayed in the spirit for years for each of these scenarios. At this time, I was a prayer coordinator at a local church and served as an International Elder interceding for people and the nation's emotions. I began to study courses and clinical counselor courses under a local healing center in Memphis, TN. Praying special prayers for people situations in the 80's and 90's traditional black churches were not prepared for this kind of ministries. Some people after going to senior pastor we would recommend local sources that were able to go the dark places in their lives. The churches neither the pastors was not equipped to handle. I was through prayer that families would open up to me about the hurt and violation of abuse that they were still experiencing. So many women, girls, boys and men are so messed up, missing the reality of enjoying life because of the shame, and the darkness of silence. Missing real love, the hidden heart that is decimated with emotions, incorruptible beauty, and quiet spirit that is valuable to God.

I began to read my journals, writings, and prayers after over 20 years plus ministry, being involved with people who were trying to recover from flashbacks or hurtful incidents that caused the pain. In this book, you will see prayers prayed for sexual abuse, molestation, rape, child abuse, domestic violence, and the forms of abuse to be healed by the Holy Spirit allowing me to feel their pain of anger, depression, and guilt feelings of never being good enough to fit in.

Matthew 8:7 - TLB

"Yes," Jesus said, "I will come and heal him."

Romans 8:26-27 - New King James Version (NKJV)

[26] Likewise, the Spirit also helps in our weaknesses. For we do not know what we should pray for as we ought, but

the Spirit Himself makes intercession for us with groaning's which cannot be uttered. [27] Now He who searches the hearts knows what the mind of the Spirit *is,* because He makes intercession for the saints according to *the will of* God.

As believers, God has valuable resources and anointed people now to help you cope with your situations and circumstances in life. Even when you do not know how to pray or what words to say, the Holy Spirit intervenes to tell God what He has said through His words. God will answer yes, no, or just a quietness. If there is just a quietness, I believe He is just saying to be still and know that I am God. You can tell when God is enabling us to pray, we feel free, we feel light, and there is peace of all understanding.

It is a book that introduces to you God is showing us that we are still missing pieces in the ministry. Churches still don't have passionate people on staff equipped to pray those special prayers in the various areas of abuse, to help people who need to come in for prayer or advocate to listen and not distribute their personal business throughout the ministry. We have to be careful of this being your call; not only does it put you in a special position for the body of Christ. But you will be held accountable to God for how you treat His people whom He entrusts you to stand in proxy with for their illness. We are missing souls in the ministry; on every pew, there are at least three or more people needing the kind of help for damaged emotions. "This happens to you" or to a family member or a friend; this is an urge of importance. It is very real; every day, the statistic is getting higher. It will take a special person, a gifted person who loves to pray at all times and doesn't mind getting in the deep for the people of

God to trust the advocate of God with their pain and hurt. Ask yourself the question: Do you have a staff member equipped to minister or pray in these areas of healing for damaged emotions, or recommend them to a minister their gift of prayer and spirit-filled to a therapist for extensive help? I would like to recommend not trying to minister to bust your ministry and wound God's people even more. When I was younger in ministry, I would tell people to try in the lane that God has anointed them. What are you saying? Everyone does not walk in the fivefold; you only may have one. When you are sick with cancer, you would not go to a chiropractor. When you have a kidney problem, you'll need an urologist. You don't need an eye doctor. I feel that the people of God should be the same way, only the best specialist in that area.

This may be your first step, second, third or fourth step: "This Happen to you" will allow you to feel the emotions of people who have or are still experiencing this hurt. It's the emotions of the people who have driven me to write this book from someone who has walked through these emotions through the view of family, victims, church members, and friends. When this happens, you are a loved one, a small child who has not had the opportunity to make up their mind about what they wanted to be because someone stole their emotions of their sexual identity. On the inside, they were not allowed to share in how their lives would be molded or the anointing of God on my life. This does not mean that we are exempted from pain, suffering, or hardship, but that God will see us through to a glorious conclusion. I love to think and believe that goodness is for all of us.

It is my prayer that these few chapters of scenarios of different prayers will help you on your path of healing and God's repair station for domestic violence, physical abuse, child abuse, sexual molestation, rape and emotional healing. Allowing the Holy Spirit to recycle and purify you back to wholeness within yourself.

I love to reach people where they are and through the simplicity of the Holy Spirit. You will see where I used gospel lyrics from spiritual songs, R&B songs, and country artists because people relate to all forms of music lyrics, and it allowed me to really put my thoughts on paper. In today's society and in ministries, you have to be open to using various tools such as the word of God and artists to help people understand the rule, which is the Word of God, through their issues, then how to apply the rule to their lives and the conclusion is healing.

"I Believe the Word of God"

Romans 8:28-29 No, a person is a Jew who is one inwardly; and circumcision is circumcision of the heart, by the Spirit, not by the written code. Such a person's praise is not from other people but from God. NIV

When looking from the outside to the inside, we do not like to talk about what is ugly and painful. We feel shame that we do not have that perfect family lives. We do everything we can to keep the outside world from knowing. In reaching deep within my heart to overcome the obstructions in my life while holding on to my impossible dream. We do not want each other to know. Therefore, we endure silence. However, the hurt is still here. Some people are suffering in their hearts. Others perpetuate deep pain upon family and peers that we declare to love. Some of us know the secrets that dwell within our homes. Then you say to yourself, "I have changed," so that all humankind could have a connection back to the fellowship and benefits of God. "For He made Him who knew no sin to be sin for us, that we might become the righteousness of God in Him" (2 Cor. 5:21). In paraphrasing this, God is saying, "Look at me, look at me for My amazing grace," I once was lost but now I'm found, I was blind, but now I see. During all those years of darkness and domestic violence, through advocacy programs for the abuse, I see with the Word of God. Believe that God's Word will pick you up when you are down, Believe that God's Word is your light in darkness, Believe Gods word is light for all to see because anything is possible when you believe.

I remember when I was young in ministry, our senior pastor would call anytime without notice on Saturday evening to ask me to preach at the first service on Sunday. A course I would always be ready because if you have a prayer life there is always a word from God. I always say drive in the lane God had given you. We have to dream the impossible dreams, while searching our hearts for every impediment of life while striving to strive to be your best at everything you do. Realizing your shining light is from God. As the lane is prayer for me this is where God has gifted me. I was praying for people with damage emotions, domestic abuse, and kids that suffered abuse. God just quicken my spirit to preach, "He's all I Need."

"I Believe the Word of God"

My pastor asked me, "What has God spoken to you about?" God had given me a Word in the 23 Psalm. As young evangelist, this would allow us the opportunity to speak before the body of Christ and sharing what the Holy Spirit has placed in our hearts. Therefore, I addressed, "He's all I need."

I begin the build my case on "He's all I need," looking at the emotional hurt that is invisible to the natural eye where you cannot see the injury or damage that has been done to the victim heart. I wanted to encourage the people of God that they are not alone. You cannot have an appearance of obedience without true obedience. I love when asked the question, what are you saying, here goes God considers our behavior under the circumstances. However, our thoughts and motives as Paul would say and I am paraphrasing is the membership in Gods family is external with internal traits. If your heart is right with God this allows you to be part of Gods family. God looks at our heart to draw his conclusion. A scenario God gave me about the heart; it acts like a car battery. If there is a dead cell in your battery, it causes the car to start slow or not enough connection to crank the car. Well when we are hurt, traumatized, or suffer any kind of abuse it cause us not to connect to God. When you have been a victim of rape, molestation, you are also subjected to physical abuse it affects your heart. It leaves a corrosion on your heart as if the life is being squeeze out of you that will allowing enough fire for charge, this is the way our hearts act when there is forgiveness, anger, of hate.

When we pray, it puts us in place to receive a spiritual shock of life from God to cleanse our hearts and our minds to match the shiny light of restoration. It allows the purity of our motives, not an alignment of our deeds to our impure motives. This is the goal that honors God and causes change, and we can hear God saying, "Look at me; those years of darkness could have caused you to become paralyzed."

A old hymn that is very powerful, yet today, "Amaze and Grace," we need this grace; how sweet the sound that saves a wretch like me, I once was lost but now I'm found, but now I see. I can hear God saying look at me, I can see the change.

"I Believe the Word of God"

After preaching this Word of God and making a corporate prayer that enough is enough before hundreds of people in this service, I received a prayer request passed to me by one of the ushers, a young woman who had been a victim of domestic violence, drugs, and sexual abuse for years and went to clubs while attending church every Sunday. This abuse pushed her into an alternative lifestyle as being in a relationship with a pastor who was the abuser. She thought she had met her knight; instead, her life went to hell. The apple looked good, but it was spoiled fruit. Now, she went from domestic violence to physical abuse by a man, causing intentional injury. No one saw or recognized her hidden abuse or pain.

I called the young woman at her request and offered an individual prayer for her situation and confidence in what was being shared. This woman was spirit-filled, anointed singer, attending church every Sunday but living in suppressed pain every. I shared with her a few weeks ago and had an ear to listen as she shared her pain. We built a trustworthy friendship and knew what she shared would be private. I wanted to know why she never received help and stayed in such an abusive relationship. No attempts to leave.

It was then that I reached out again through prayer and a recommendation for medical and mental help. I always made the senior pastor aware of this situation. When working with people in abusive situations, emotional or child abuse, child, adult or infant, you have to report and document these incidents in case there is legal repercussion against your minister later on. I walked this woman into a treatment and drug detox center. Because the treatment center was only for 30 days, this was a first step for her but she needed more treatment. At this time in ministry, the churches were not set up to help her in this situation.

Domestic violence is a very serious abuse that still goes unreported, and it is not a quick fix. The percentage of people sitting in the pews or chairs with this kind of pain, asking who can I trust in this house of God to help me? Ask yourself if you have the gift to help these victims. This is a slow process, and a very special person can handle these kinds of problems and direction to believe there is healing.

"I Believe the Word of God"

I believe in the Word of God. Keep Believing. Do not stop praying and believing! This is the most common reason why some people do not receive healing. People will become discouraged and give up their faith. Most are looking for microwave rapid healing, but most healings occur gradually and piece by piece throughout time. We have to be patient and be faithful in our spirit. Keep on praising and giving thanks to Him for our answer. God's will be faithful unto his word; if you will be true to believe! "...Do not become sluggish, but imitate those who through faith and patience inherit the promises" (Hebrews 6:12).

I believe God's Word over domestic violence, I believe God's word over my pain, over my emotions, never to leave me or forsake me, I believe the blood of Jesus over everything, amen.

Prayer for Domestic Violence

Father, in the name of Jesus, help me to love my enemies and pray for those who persecute you. O God, help me to do good to those who hate you; help me to pray for those who abused me. Bless those who curse you and Father, in the name of Jesus, the abuser.

Oh, Father, I believe your Words about domestic violence, physical abuse, and emotional damage. I believe in God over my pain. I believe that God will never leave us or forsake us. I believe in the blood of Jesus. Holy Spirit, thank you for weeping in the night, and joy is coming in the morning.

God of peace, Father, I pray for women and families that do not have peace. Father, in the name of Jesus, there are many women who are weighed down with the fear of violence, the after-effects of this abuse.

Father, I asked in my closing request for total healing to their minds, body and spirits, in Jesus' name. Amen

"Be Safe"

Proverbs 18:10: the name of the LORD is a fortified tower; the righteous run to it and are safe. NIV

<u>Psalms 23:1- 4</u>

The Lord is my shepherd, I lack nothing. [2] He makes me lie down in green pastures, he leads me beside quiet waters, 3 he refreshes my soul. He guides me along the right paths for his name's sake. NIV

Today, we have so many friends, family, churches, schools, and peers that have such dysfunctional acts within the places that should be safe. Take a safe touch, an unsafe touch, or an unwanted touch. Child molestation and child abuse are again on the rise if they ever stop. In case studies, the first words are, you're not telling the truth, no one has time to listen to you, and no one cares because the knock is not at your door or there is no one to relieve your anxiety. Then we attack God; *how could you allow this to happen, and you say that you love me? How can you expect me to forgive someone who has violated me or violated my child?* Your child that has been involved in sexual activities to perform sexual gratification to a perpetrator, a statutory rape, or other sexual exploitative activities. Statistics say that 1 in 4 girls and 1 in 6 boys will be sexually abused before the age of 18 years old. It is through God's Word that Jesus prayed, "Father, forgive them," because He was fulfilling Old Testament prophecy: "He bore the sin of many, and made intercession for the transgressors" (Isaiah 53:5). From the cross, Jesus interceded for sinners. On the cross, Jesus provided forgiveness for all those who would ever believe in Him. (Matthew 20:28). Jesus paid the penalty for the sins that we committed in our ignorance and even the ones we have committed deliberately.

Young people are saying "be safe" in their conversations with each other, with their families ensuring them of being safe while at school, in colleges, trying to avoid being sexually assaulted on college campuses, and children walking home from school.

Another prayer request from a family within the church for their niece and nephew who at 12 years of age and were victims of child abuse, child neglect, and sexual assault. At this time, I was serving as a youth advisor receiving another prayer request doing bible study. I let them speak freely in their own words. The younger sister said, "I do not believe in God," and the young boy said, "Where was God when he allowed our uncle to molest us from five years old to age 11 years old." The prayer request was so graphic details of uncle performing oral acts on both of them. Uncle used his hands in unwanted touching on the private parts of their bodies.

I am glad you asked the question: Where was the mother? These kids were born into a dysfunctional family where the mother was a drug addict and physically abused, living in the streets in the urban area of Tennessee. The mother died, and the kids were taken in by their maternal aunt. The aunt was a member of the church I was attending, and this is how I met them. I was teaching the youth on this Wednesday night, and I had a basket when they came in and placed their prayer request. This was kept private to their prayer requests. The brother and sister asked for prayer for their family and starting over after the decease of their mother.

We were preparing for a skit, "O behold the Lamb, now behold the Lamb, the precious Lamb of God, and born into sin that I may live again, the precious Lamb of God," using the arrangement of Kirk Franklin. This skit was with praise dancers and a dramatic scene of the cross. The young boy was playing Jesus on the cross. While playing the role of Jesus on the cross, he experienced an emotional breakdown. As the kids were trying to take his body from the cross, this young boy froze with emotions. I walked over to him and asked what was wrong. I will never forget that moment; those were tears of real pain, and his body was pale and speechless. As the music continued to play softly in taking down, we took him to the back as his aunt met me in the rear of the church. Asking their permission if she wanted me to pray or try to question, he began to calm down but still crying with no hope. Thinking to me, *My God, My God, how could this kind of violence and abuse happen?*

What is happening here? As I began to pray and his aunt was holding his hands while they were traumatized as well, his face was flushed, and he was crying outrageously. The aunt was shocked and did not know what to say or do. As I remained calm by the Holy Spirit, and still praying in a calm tone of voice. He began to speak slowly and softly; his broken memories by of his sister, who had died in a car accident, and the inappropriate gestures his uncle did to him and his sisters as children, in his mind, were on the cross.

I asked in a still, quiet voice. "Do you mean the cross," he said. However, what he was describing was a scarecrow. Scarecrow-like people built-in fields to keep the birds away. It was not the cross but through a child's eyes and remembering the shape of the cross or scarecrow. The cross-triggered the painful memory, pain that wretched hours that he even wanted to die, commit suicide. His sister had died the previous year in a car accident. In addition, he felt that he could no longer live, the secret was out. The aunts got him into therapy and into the doctor's office to be, examined, showing that he had been a victim of rape and child molestation and he had become a repeated offender to his cousin. He was in therapy, but it was not enough. He was fighting the emotions, trying to fight the urgencies of sexual drive for kids, as a defender. We need more help for domestic violence, physical abuse, and damage emotions. Unfortunately, there were not enough trained people or facilities can meet the people's needs.

I begin to pray in the spirit. Lord, I look to you for guidance on what is happening here and what is going on in his mind on the cross. The word of God says, "If you refuse to take up your cross and follow me, you're not worthy of being mine." (Matthew 10:38) NIV. I believe that this was saying, take up your cross and follow Jesus, trusting him we can lay down our cares and urgencies and become committed to Christ. We should be totally committed to Christ. We should be completely committed to God, Facing anything even suffering as death for sake.

My senior pastor returned, and of course, I shared with him what was happening with this young person and his aunts. I accompanied them to the emergency hospital because there was another case of suicide and incident that needed to be documented with the authorities. I am reminded of the word in the bible: is there not a cause? Yes, there is a cause to put an end to child abuse and emotional trauma. He received emergency care that night and I recommended that she get him into therapy so he can share all his emotions and fears. I followed him and his family for about three more years to his 18th birthday.

He continued treatment, but when he reached 18 years, he came out of the closet to his family. He thought enough to call me and say thank you for praying for me as a kid. He said so much, this happen to him in life, and this is a hard disease to fight. In the conversation, he said, "Elder, I did not ask for this."

I believe the Word of God completely, but I do not have a heaven or hell to put you in or anyone else. I hope that this story will help those families that do not know how to love their child through child abuse or are too ashamed to get help for them that you let them fall. There are local resources in your cities. If you do not get what you need from one, keep trying. God has someone assigned to tarry with you for your healing, but do not give up.

Prayer for Child Molestation

Holy Spirit, I pray for your endless love for the children and families that have experienced child molestation. God, I pray for the two hearts that beat as one, but yet there is an irregular heartbeat.

Father, we pray for a spiritual blood transfusion to restore and purify the emotions. Lord, heal that emotional look in their eyes when all they want is to be happy again. O God, secure life and hope for that child that has been violated. Father, as I call upon the name of Jesus each day, you will pull the victim out of the pit and set their life on a new, unshakeable path. Thank you, Holy Spirit, for new dreams and vision. Amen

Shadows of Darkness

He reveals the deep things of darkness and brings utter darkness into the light. Jobs 12:22 NIV

There are many ministries that have not yet addressed domestic violence, child abuse, physical and emotional abuse, and suicide because you do not know what true story of a victim that is sitting in the pews and stairs. "I Didn't Ask For This" is not to bring solidity to anyone's ministries but to bring healing to the holistic body of Christ. Dark shadow refers to domestic abuse, child abuse, and physical and emotional abuse, which is a dark area where a dense victim blocks light from a light source. It inhabits a three-dimensional book behind a piece with light in front of it. When the emotional light is reflecting on a victim of domestic violence, sexual assault, or child abuse, this turns all the dimensions of your shadow on. This comes by the way of fear and emotions of feeling ashamed. People who have experienced these emotions, whether it was in their homes, growing up as a child, or being abused in a relationship. Maybe you shared this with your mother, who did not believe you. Alternatively, you might have masked your violence with a smile, singing while passing a prayer request to an intercessor for prayer.

The churches are one of the essential ventures that all walks of people will enter into. We must have gifted people who will sincerely pray for these people's requests. It is a 911 that centers and churches become more equipped to assist the people of God, whether it is through a small cell group. A light of reality concerning domestic violence, sexual assault and the other areas of abuse is a critical step in keeping or preventing people from going to that dark place. Now, we will create a pathway to safety for the victims and family members that are critical.

It is essential that people continually speak out about the different abuses and silent violations of God's love that can give victims the strength to seek a better way. It will allow them the freedom of being bound, chains holding their shadow of emotions in darkness. Victims will be able to break the codes of silence and break the generational cycles of repeated abuse. If we have more churches and initiative programs collaborating in unity, this will help the holistic body to be healthier. Speak it so that men, women, young adults and celebrities will sow financial gifts. There are other programs in cities and countries that they perform in accepting to help transform the world, healing their low self-esteem, paralyzing their potential, their low esteem, and sabotaging your Christian services.

Here is another scenario for a young woman that I met at church and the community choir we both sang in. I noticed the bruises, the dark marks on her arms, and the broken eyeglasses. She would cry uncontrollably every Sunday as if there were no hope for the domestic violence that she was enduring. She was very fearful and ashamed of her six-month-old son at the time. Her husband had been in and out of jail for domestic charges and other offenses. I was serving as a prayer coordinator. Here again, this young woman heard me speak on "It's Time To Grow," and I was addressing all acts of physical, sexual, and psychological violence using the principles of God's word. The anointing of God had set the atmosphere, standing still until God's will for her life became clear. It was an encounter with the Holy Spirit for her; she had received an email right then. It was as if she wanted to, and did, give her heart to God, who was her friend. Violence will disappear from your land — all war will end. Your walls will be "Salvation," and your gates "Praise." Isaiah 60:18

Here comes the prayer request as I was allowed to pray a corporate prayer for that body of Christ, and lifting up emotionally damaged people and trusting the Holy Spirit for restorations and healing. As I reached out to the young woman during the week, she trusted God's anointing on my life and began to open up. I listened to what she had to say about being molested as a child and other acts of sexual abuse by family members as well. She mentioned her relationship with her mother was much strained, and she never would believe her. There was a deep anger against her mother. Because of her level of faith, I was able to reach her heart. God sees our hearts at all times, and he knows if it is working properly. One thing I told her is that you have to start with forgiveness, and that should start with your mother. Will it be easy? No, but we only have one mother. Her husband was incarcerated at the time. She heard that her husband was being released in a few weeks, which pushed her into PTS (Posttraumatic Stress). With all of this emotional, domestic abuse, low self-esteem, lack of trust with her family, there was an attempt of suicide.

She called late in the evening, and I could tell by her voice that something was not right. I got in my car and drove to her small apartment. As I entered, I saw pills on the floor and her six-month-old son sitting on the floor crying. I immediately called 911 and then her grandmother. At this time, I did what I knew best; I took her in my arms and the baby in my other arms. In addition, I began to call on the name of Jesus, walking back and forth. I began to petition for healing, the God of repentance, and to restore and heal this vessel for this baby. It was a war cry. The ambulance arrived and took her to the ER trauma center, and a rough 48 hours were critical. By this time, her family had made it to the ER. I began, in the ER waiting room, to go into warfare for my friend's life. Again, God heard me; He saved her life, and she went into treatment. She was able to get the help in therapy and through support groups that she needed. I thank God; he restored her relationship with her mother. Nothing is like a mother's love.

As she got better each day, she was at the point where she wanted to be healed totally through every emotion and restoration in her heart, knowing that God could then touch the heart of the aggressor through the Holy Spirit. The process begins when the victim's pain and physical healing can release forgiveness for the abuser, a pain that was so intense as a woman's water during childbirth breaks.

When God shines his light of life on the shadows of death, yes, though I walk through the valley of the shadow of death, I will fear no evil: for You are with me, Your rod and Your staff, they comfort me.

Death casts the most frightening shadow that has covered every area of our lives, making us most helpless when it prevents itself. We, as humans, struggle with many emotions of pain, suffering, doubt, forgiveness, and shame until we get to a place of pressing into the heart of Jesus. As the healing begins, you find yourself using the name of Jesus more, entrusting yourself into His hands. Saying His name so that you now believe that justice will take place, and in the name of Jesus, the power of darkness is over. The shadow of the cross allows you to say, "I entrust my heart, my spirit, and my soul into the hands and heart of God."

When you minister to people with this kind of abuse, pain, and injuries, you have to remind them that you may not see Him in nature, but I can assure you He is on the scene at all times. Even when you are in your darkest hour and the lowest valley, you are able to feel Him. It is like the thermostat on the wall that directs heat when it is cold but cannot be seen, and then it gives you cool air when it is too high. You can choose the signal, but you cannot see it, and that is what God does for us. He is fixing your broken heart and healing your bruises.

Prayer for Suicidal Attempt

Father, in the name of Jesus, I pray for _______ in this suicidal attempt. Father, I pray for the doctors, the nurses, and the staff that come in contact with her. Oh, Father, I ask for forgiveness on her behalf for the suicidal attempt to take her life. I stand in proxy on her behalf until you restore her to her right mind. Father, my prayer is for her infant son and the family as you give them guidance in approaching you. Father, I am asking for the dispatch of her assigned angel to intervene in this situation. Holy Spirit, breathe life into this fragile body. In addition, regulate all of her vitals to line up with your healing power. In Jesus' name, Amen.

Pray

44 But I say to you, love your enemies, bless those who curse you, do good to those who hate you, and pray for those who spitefully use you and persecute you. (Matthew 5:44) NKJV

Fathers, do not provoke your children to anger but bring them up in the discipline and instruction of the Lord. (Ephesians 6:4) ESV

We now have GPS; we can google driving directions about, how we can ask God for directions of our children. Father, you take control; take it out of my hands because I cannot handle the pathway of the family. Nurturing our kids to follow Christ is a lot like trying to navigate depending on GPS in underdeveloped road contractions. Have you ever been in a city and you have the GPS that you have programmed for the directions, but you run into a road detour, and the GPS has sent you one hundred miles out of the way? We head in the direction that seems best, trying to find our way by trial and error. Well, this happens sometimes, and we try to raise our kids in the best way to become vibrant followers of Christ, but life brings incidents and trials that we never thought would affect our family.

I named this chapter "Pray" while I was thinking about the children who had experienced child abuse, physical and sexual abuse. Not life has brought so many endless interruptions. As I have wrestled with indecisiveness and self-doubt, I have sought God's Word for help. "Show me the right path, O LORD; point out the road for me to follow.

Lead me by your truth and teach me, for you are the God who saves me. All day long I put my hope in you" (Psalm 25:4-5).

In looking at Matthew 5 chapter, Jesus is asking not to retaliate for injustice. Well, the scripture is easier said than done when your child has been violated. What God is saying is to love and pray for your enemies rather than retaliate. This is a healing process, and it does not happen overnight. At this time, you are praying for a broken heart that is crushed into pieces; your pain is so intense that you are asking God to breathe for you. Justin Bieber came out with a song called "Pray" that speaks to kids with so many emotions — broken hearts, breathing problems, and unrecognizable pain. In paraphrasing, we can only overcome the pain, abuse, and emotions through a relationship with God; only He can deliver people from their own selfishness. Praying and depending on the Holy Spirit to comfort, heal, and help us love kids and families in times like these when you don't feel that love for now.

At this time, I was now working at a difference ministry and still driving in the lane that God had gifted me in "Prayer." I was sitting at work, and my pastor called me to place a two-year-old little girl on the prayer list for having a heart transplant. While speaking to the pastor and adding the little girl's name to the prayer list for a heart transplant. I mentioned to him that a church member had sent a prayer request for her two-year-old son, who had been sexually molested by an older cousin. In addition, he replied all right. A week or two had passed, and the pastor followed up to see if we still had the family lifted up with the two-year-old daughter's heart transplant. My prayer for this little girl was God would heal her totally, praying that the heart would not reject her body. Praying that there be no infection in her blood, that the blood will be pure and that there are no blood clots. In addition, God will give her parents the faith of a mustard seed to believe in God for total healing. I thank God the report is she was recovering as expected from her surgeon.

I reminded the pastor that we still had the two-year-old boy still on the prayer list and believed in God for his healing from molestation and abuse. I told the pastor that his mother said he was having nightmares and sweating on the bed. In addition, he was very fearful. I told my pastor I was trying to stay focused. I was a little angry because this child's innocence had been violated. My pastor never responded to what had happened to this little boy. I began to pray and fast because it bothered me that the senior pastor did not offer a parent for this little boy. As I continued to pray and seek God, why did the pastor not offer prayer for this little boy? People that have that gift of discerning visions and dreams God will reveal. I heard God speak clearly, saying he could not pray for this little boy at this time because; he had been violated as a child.

I recommended getting her son examined and recommended a child advocacy center. My first concern was to offer a treatment advocacy center for her son and to keep the cousin separated from him. This was rape; molestation of a child had to be reported as a crime. Here, the initiative was to direct the mother to the relevant people, such as the police department, who told her the same thing, recommending the child to an advocacy center to help children become kids again. Teaching kids sexual abuse is never the child's fault.

As for the pastor, I cannot say he prayed for the boy, but it brought back memories of his violation and someone he looked up to. I had completed the intervention there and got the child and his mother the family needed. The pastor was not a repeated offense, but it is painful to face emotions when you think you have been healed years ago. It was my prayer that God would restore and heal him from those emotions of shame, fear, and pain. Fear can cause us to put up barriers, and pride can do it as well. God has anointed psychologists, therapists, and counselors who have been chosen and appointed to treat you holistically. It is through their help and the guidance of God that we can diffuse low self-esteem and shame and learn how to trust again. We have centers in our community where children are safe, families are strong, and victims become children again. Their mission is to serve children who are victims of sexual and severe physical abuse through prevention, education, and intervention. In addition, it is the profits from this book that will enable me to keep this center alive.

Another scenario is about a ten-year-old girl whom I met while her mother now incarcerated but, at the time, was living with a live-in boyfriend who was not the father. I was working with the grandmother, who had custody of the kids. It was time for this little girl's wellness checkup. We had a power of attorney in place to help them while she was incarcerated on several charges, one being child neglect. He performed her wellness checkup, and because of the molestation, they had to do the pelvic exam. The doctor asked if he could speak to the little girl with the female nurse. He talked about good touch and bad touch. The doctor came out, and he took me to another room with the head doctor. They asked me and her grandmother if we knew she had been molested. Our answers were both no, and the doctors explained to her what she had told him and the nurse because she was a minor and in the custody of her grandmother at the time. Before going back into the room with the young girl, we were taken to another room, briefing us on what had been developed. Now, we are back in the room with the young girl, and medical officials recommend her for immediate therapy through the child advocacy center. I tried to remain calm, but my emotions were all over the place. To hear a 10-year-old girl give such a graphic description, sleeping problem, fighting in her sleep, sexual behavior, the knowledge that was so inappropriate, making the child touch his genitals, she was doing self-mutilations to herself and inappropriately watching her undress or use the bathroom. She suffered sudden unexplained personality changes and mood swings and seemed insecure. She had been exposed to domestic violence, living below poverty and learning disability and told the doctor that she wanted to take her life in committing suicide.

As we began to leave the building, she was crying, her heart was beating fast, and she was choking in her speech, saying, "Why did this happen to me?" I hug her and tell her that I love her, God loves her, and I will try to help get this fixed so she would not have to go through this again. No child should ever have to be subject to this kind of violation. She lays her head on my shoulder, and I say, "I feel good being around you." In my mind, I am praying all the time, "Father, touch this child today; give her a touch to make her feel like she is safe in your arms." God, in the name of Jesus, please make a miracle out of this tragedy. It reminds me of Yolanda Adams with a song that resonated in my spirit, "What About the Children?" Yes, another child sexual abuse case.

We were able to get her into treatment for kids at the child advocacy center. She had to give a video statement at this center. After a complete investigation, they put in a child protection order, and charges were brought against the abuser. He is still in court for this incident. The mother is incarcerated for various charges and child neglect. She is now in the custody of her grandmother, and I try to offer assistance as much as I can. This is another proven factor that we still do not have enough help within the community or the finances to support these programs. We have programs that feed over 3,000 kids per week, but what about these families that are sitting on somebody's pews each week crying in silence? Schools fall short in their social services; the symptoms are there to push these issues because they do not want to be involved. While each day, the statistic is growing in child abuse, domestic violence, and untouched emotions waiting to be healed, every 24 minutes, people are victims of rape, molestation, and domestic violence in a year's time.

Prayer – For Sexually Abused Kids

God, I come before you today on behalf of kids and families of sexual abuse. I pray for total healing. I pray for the comfort in their souls. I pray, God, that You can lead them to a new place in their lives, guiding them with your grace, Father, in the name of Jesus, restore the purity and memories of being a kid that has been stolen. Their innocent and brokenness in the families, O God, I put it in Your hands; it's too big for us. Father, direct us to the road of healing that seems hopeless, that has shattered dreams and a path for healing. I commend You on the authority of Jesus Christ. Father, You take this wheel and align our mind, body, and spirit with your love in saving us with your compensatory excellence. Amen.

"Broken Pieces"

Jeremiah 17:14 God, pick up the pieces of my life. Put me back together again. I give you my praise.

Psalms 147:3 3 He heals the brokenhearted and binds up their wounds.

There will be days when it seems your life is broken into so many pieces: pieces of sadness, pieces of sickness, pieces of emotional stress, and now suffering from broken hearts. This is a scenario of spiritual violation within a ministry. While it may not manifest as physical rape, the signs and symptoms parallel the emotional violation indicative of abuse. Attempting to listen to your favorite song reveals a changed experience; the lyrics of Kelly Clarkson's "Piece by Piece" resonate in your spirit: "He'll never walk away, He'll love me, Piece by Piece, he will restore your faith." This marks a season of breaking the generational cycle of physical, verbal, and emotional abuse. 20 Though you have made me to see troubles, many, you will restore my life again; from the depths of the earth will again bring me up. 21 You will increase my honor and comfort me once more. (Psalms 70: 20-21)

Life can sometimes leave you feeling tired as it passes you by in slow motion while your world seems to have lost its flavor. You do not hear music the way you used to; you do not see clouds the way you used to. The sweet aroma of fresh fallen rain that used to delight your senses now goes by overlooked as lifeless floods that dampen your frame of mind. Life will make you ask the question, "How can you mean this broken heart?" The bible says there is a time to live and a time to die. Therefore, through this Word, God will give you a dose of joy that gives insight into our purpose. The ministry of music of healing directs us to handle life circumstances. Tunes come on the radio, such as "Jesus Takes the Wheel" by Carrie Underwood, asking for directions and the weakness of not being able to hold on to life situations; it could be domestic violence, emotional stress, or raped in the spirit.

If I were to express my viewpoints at this time, it would involve grappling with the past hurt experienced in the church, where thoughts and opinions about wrong actions within God's house are swallowed. Witnessing adultery acts within the ministry marked a fall from grace for the pastor. It happened on a Friday during prayer when the Lord allowed me to speak to three brothers in the ministry. A simple word from God urged them to step away from the pastor and seek God in their marriages. Little did I know one of the guys in the ministry was the intended recipient of this prophetic word.

Every Sunday, week after week, I observed the pain in the eyes of the first lady, rendered speechless by the prestige, power, and position of our senior pastor's immoral actions. I distinctly recall stating that I don't have the authority to assign individuals to heaven or hell. However, I couldn't ignore the fact that these actions, emanating from the head of the ministry, were perpetuating toxic faith practices.

I firmly believe that leaders overseeing the souls of men, women, boys, and girls while serving God — the Father, Son, and Holy Spirit — will be held accountable for actions outside God's will. My gift lies in intercessory prayer, and through this, God reveals these toxic spirits. The weight of prayer is, at times, overwhelming, causing physical discomfort. In prayer, God unveiled the spirit of Jezebel that had consumed the ministry.

Women were just finding their place in the ministry, engaging in immoral acts and standing in front of the congregation to preach but not being well-received. The old cliché "what's done in the dark will come to light" proved true as a woman became pregnant by another preacher assigned to the youth. Numerous women in the congregation showed disrespect, including towards the first lady. The pastor, elevated in control, created an environment where one felt the need for his approval and validation to be part of the ministry. Opinions and perceptions of wrong actions were not welcomed.

The Jezebel spirit in the ministry was prevalent, extending its influence to the church. Staff members misappropriated church funds before proper recording, and church credit cards were misused for personal gain. Young girls became pregnant by older men of honor, leading to fights among their children who, as they grew older, understood their father's immoral actions with women in the church. Such actions caused pain for their mothers. Deacons fathered children outside their families, and couples broke up, contributing to a rise in divorces.

Being part of a ministry like this crushed my heart; I didn't fit in and experienced verbal abuse. One young minister, serving as an adjutant to the senior pastor, fell into darkness, committing adultery with another woman and fathering a son with her, just a year younger than his daughter from his wife. His wife discovered this outside son while out with their daughter and her husband. The little boy recognized his father, ran over, and hugged him around the legs. Within weeks, the same minister left for Chicago with another pregnant woman, intending to have her abort the baby.

The list of depression and disappointments seeking healing from a higher power continued. I cried out to God, reaching out to Him. Through a spiritual encounter, I felt God taking control of all these situations without hesitation. Feeling lost in the church and thinking survival was impossible, I discovered that crying out to God and embracing hopelessness with a belief to receive resonated in my heart. It became evident that the hope God provides can heal broken pieces, including the heart, spirit, and soul.

As evangelists and ministers, we were dedicated servants to the ministry financially, serving in the ministry, speaking, and evangelizing in building the kingdom of God.

I was hurt in a car accident in 2000 and was not able to be in service. God took this time to heal my mind, body and soul in being subjected to all the immoral acts. I was serving as the prayer coordinator. Due to my injuries, I was not able to be at church, so God gave me the idea to have prayer over the phone; we connected the team in three ways at the time. The senior pastor said this was not enough, her wanted people that their in the building praying. Long story short I had a young woman working with me, but this young woman was not gifted in this area of ministry or a leader. She was given this position because it was a have and have not. I was a young evangelist who operated in the anointing. She was very nice young women that had the money and he wanted to impress one of his deacon with prestige, power, and position. She was not able to hold that ministry together, this was a form of riding on another peorson anointing. To make this even clearer in the bible and they serached out David among his brothers becsue he carried the anointing on his life. I was going through the process of healing in my body.

I had undergone six surgeries, and the senior pastor had thrown me away like an old shirt. He was a charismatic leader that would pull you away from Grace to follow his laws. If you had an opinion of not going along with him he would label you as "unsub missive," or you would be preached at from the pulpit in a bulling style and now you are on his bad side. Abuse from the leader and daring other leaders and members not to speak of to you. Now saying you are weak and has emotional issues. I desired to live a christ life but to be subjected to hold all of this conruption was to much. As young people today say, "you think." You do not think that this happens in God House but it does. Another area I serve in this ministry was a writer for the church gazette paper, none of the other ministers wanted to write.

The editor had assigned me a section to write on the topic of "healing for damaged emotions," specifically for Ministers in Training (MIT). However, the senior pastor instructed the editor to discontinue my writing. Despite adhering to biblical principles and applying the word of God, the senior pastor alleged that I was attempting to self-promote through my writing. This idea had never crossed my mind; I was simply utilizing the gift that God had bestowed upon me. Due to a lack of willing ministers, the church paper was eventually discontinued.

The emotional impact felt akin to being raped or violated in God's house. Spiritual abuse, often labeled as witchcraft, tends to go unrecognized. The pastor harbored a jealous spirit, utilizing worldly agendas within the church. This led to the blocking of future speaking engagements, prompting my decision to leave. After enduring such abusive treatment in ministry, God granted me the strength to depart and seek healing for myself — a form of abuse that made me question the increasing breakdown of marriages, the prevalence of inappropriate relationships with the youth, and the exodus from the ministry.

As God opened my eyes, I felt blind and bound to silence. The trauma from this abuse profoundly affected my physical and spiritual life, dismantling my peace of faith. I was cast aside, shamed, and shattered. In the last fifteen years, the ministry has lacked consistency in the area of prayer. Reflecting on the story of King David falling into bed with Bathsheba, it becomes clear how individuals in leadership can succumb to moral failings.

I had to run for my life. My healing came through the Word, "Do not touch my anointed ones; do my prophets no harm." Psalms 105:10 NIV

When the head of a ministry falls from the grace of God, engaging in ungodly acts along with the leaders under him, it becomes a form of spiritual control abuse. God's message doesn't endorse blindly following the life of a prophet verbatim. Some ministries wield this power to make dissent uncomfortable within the ranks. I firmly believe that people attend church or serve in a ministry not to engage in conflict. While no church is perfect, God's Word allows us the right to hold our own opinions.

When leaders fall from grace, they should take responsibility for their wrongdoings without dragging others into their weaknesses. I stand on the word of God, recognizing that it doesn't give the right to slander a man or woman of God. When God called, appointed, and anointed me, He was restoring my faith, piece by piece, to live and not die.

Those who have experienced spiritual abuse in the church share symptoms akin to physical abuse, verbal abuse, and low self-esteem. God places people to help with emotional, economic, and psychological aspects when a spiritual leader tries to suppress thoughts and paralyze facts. My connection with the victims' hurt and pain was through prayer, realizing that I had been subjected to emotional damage by the church. God allowed me to physically feel each scenario as a healing tool, understanding the pain of each victim and praying for their survival.

Many milestones of healing remain uncharted, and numerous people are still lost due to insufficient support for their healing. Women, kids, and families are forced to endure violent situations because shelters impose restrictions on acceptance rather than addressing the core issue of healing. Single mothers with five or more kids are denied entry due to family size. Boys aged 11 and older are prohibited in centers, leading to separation from their mothers. Shelters offer limited programs, often just a week or thirty days, perpetuating the separation. Victims, whether women in years of domestic violence or young college students seeking extended help, often face unrealistic expectations to turn their lives around in a short time.

As believers, it's time to incorporate prayer leaders who can multitask and go the extra mile to find centers, shelters, and programs for these families.

God placed a wonderful social worker in my life who believed in the healing power of the word of God. As I worked through church hurt and sought healing for my soul, body, and spirit, she guided me through the scriptures, helping me articulate and address these emotions. Piece by piece, she assisted in restoring me. This process taught me to break the cycle of distorted emotions in life. It was in this space that I learned to trust Jesus for complete healing and protection, relinquishing control and allowing God's justice, balance, and rewards to prevail by making Him my choice.

Often, we distance ourselves from God because trust in the church or ministry has eroded. Faced with advice to stay silent and lacking support from family, one can feel stuck. However, we should not underestimate God's ability to take our hearts and scars. Delving into chapters and verses, I sought to break the cycles of generational abuses, activating faith in God working on my behalf behind the scenes. Though unseen, His presence is felt, much like the thermostat on the wall signaling temperature changes — you can't see it but feel it. When the right song resonates, God releases healing, love, and faith through the lyrics.

Emotional healing requires the right words of God to penetrate your bloodstream, akin to seeking a medical physician and therapist for God's health plan for your broken pieces. Maintaining a relationship with my therapist and viewing God as my specialist in hurt and pain, I break the cycle not just for myself but for a world grappling with depression, emotional damages, healing from distress, and restoration in the heart. Through this bond, I've recommended many to her, believing that God has assigned good therapy for each individual. Seeking God in prayer and meditation for His promises, even in the depths of adversity, is a reminder that God is just a prayer away.

Prayer for Damage Emotion

Heavenly Father, I pray today for your healing touch on my deep emotions. I pray for the emotional pain that I've experienced in this spiritual rape of my anointing. Thank you for allowing me to come into repentance for the forgiveness of my wounded emotions in my wounded heart. Father, as you come into my heart, which only you can see and bind up the brokenness inside. Thank you for your healing love, Lord; thank you for breaking the cycles, breaking the chains, when you have no one to confide in because no one understands this kind of pain inside me. Lord, I trust you to put these pieces together and make me hold again. Father, thank you for allowing me to be healed of these damaged emotions. Amen.

Loud and Clear

4 Fathers, do not provoke your children to anger, but bring them up in the discipline and instruction of the Lord. Ephesians 6:4 English Standard Version (ESV)

Well, when people reach the peak of this book, it will direct them on the road of domestic abuse, rape, child molestation, physical abuse and emotional abuse like the kaleidoscope of life. While writing this book, I have multiple cases of abuse. It reminds me of a kaleidoscope that was invented in the 19th century by Sir David Brewster. He named it after two Greek words meaning 'beautiful' and 'form' and added the word scope to show that it was something that you look through. It is a tube lined with mirrors set at angles to each other. The end will have patterns on it, but it should let light through. This is what God is doing through healing in each scenario of abuse as the result of past hurts and pain.

As the Holy Spirit leads, guides, and directs me to write a process of healing for women, college students, kids and families, the word abuse describes mistreatment and abuse of trust and objectives. Forms of mistreatment in domestic violence, rape and children can be physical abuse, sexual abuse, emotional abuse and neglect. In case studies, examples of these abuses are beatings, slapping or hitting, sexual abuse in the forms of penetration, foundling, incest, and touching private areas. It is time to come out of your comfort zone and make this a part of educating women, kids, students and families about abuse, and it is not the kids' or individual fault for people to treat anyone this way. Sometimes, families miss the signs of sexual or domestic abuse in terms of knowledge of sexual acts and the deep fear of a particular person or family member. Children college students do not have the responsibility for the abuse suffered. Therefore, it is important to try to get them into a treatment program quickly that offers the follow-up for total healing. Younger kids without proper treatment tend to often carry the effects into their adult lives by becoming repeat offenders or repeating patterns. College students do not heal holistically because we are looking at the outside, not the crushed emotions that are still broken. While too many people, children are abused in different ways. I remember a conference that I was speaking at for women, and it was "Looking for love in the wrong places, there is no place for unrighteous or controlling anger in believers' or non-believers' lives, but there's hope."

Parents should seek spiritual guidance of their culture as well as counseling, asking God to direct them to a person that believes in holistically healing. God will guide them through prayer healing for that young girl who violated her on a college campus, women who are in domestic violence or the small angels that have been violated as a result of domestic violence or child neglect and all scared with emotional damage. Sometimes, through the wrong help or wrong facilities, they do not receive the right counseling, and they are damaged again. We have to be submissive to the Holy Spirit for guidance, for the right people that reach into the root of the abuse. Help these people set goals and strive for total healing. It is like an infection into an open wound, and if it is not treated properly, it damages other organs in your body.

Another prayer request from a mother of five for her kids and trying to get out of domestic violence. This woman was a victim of three generations of curses of sexual violence. It started with her grandmother, who died of domestic violence. Her mother, being raised by her grandparents, was a victim of child molestation; as she grew older, then raped and became a prostitute. She had a dysfunctional lifestyle and ended up pregnant with two kids, a girl and a boy. She then was engaged in a domestic violence relationship with her kid's father. She was in a family that was rooted in drugs, prostitution, domestic violence, and blended families in the house. Now, her daughter became a victim of child molestation at nine years old. The young girl did go to counseling, but it was not enough to be broken, violated and abused. Repeating the same things of child negligence, her daughter was molested at ten years old by her live-in boyfriend and blended family. You have to be prayerful about whom you are placing over your children in these blended families. She had a live-in boyfriend who was now abusing her 10-year-old daughter.

The mother is now incarcerated for illegal acts and separated from her kids. During this time of incarceration of the mother, the children were placed in foster care. The young girl at 10 years old needed to go in for her wellness check-up. The foster care advocate had a power of attorney in place so the child good be taken for her wellness check-up. During this wellness check-up, the little girl told the doctor and nurse that she was being sexually molested. After completing and medical examination, it was evidence that she was being raped and violated by her live-in boyfriend. By this time, being there with the grandmother of the kids, the necessary people with the police had been notified. While sitting there with the grandmother, and listened to this small girl speak about the foul acts that this man had done to her. My heart was crushed into a thousand pieces. I sit with my face, trying not to show my anger and hurt for this child. I was praying to my God, "My God, how could this be? But it happens every day." I prayed for the guidance of the Holy Spirit or how and what to say. Her description of the boyfriend touching, foundling. Placing her in abusive acts was sick. After a thorough medical examination, it was confirmed by the Child Advocacy Centre for Children that she had been molested and threatened suicide attempt.

While the hospital was making a prevision for her treatment, she was placed in my home for a while. As we drove home with her grandmother along with me, she laid her head on my shoulder and said thank you. She was crying emotionally, but she was receiving a release of pain. She said I do not feel like I want to die. I was able to tell someone, and I do not think he can hurt me. I know the Holy Spirit guided me to write this book, "This Happen to You."

Again, through the lyrics of another song by Yolanda Adams and Donnie McClurkin, who had been a victim of sexual abuse as a child. The songs clearly ask the question "What About the Children recorded in (2012) along with the Tenors. The bible gives us a practical guide to child-rearing. To train a child the way he or she should go, even when he or she is old, they will not depart from it.

Therefore, 'This Happen to You' is a compelling book with a pressing mission to reach nations as an instructive guide, offering invaluable insights for children, college students, ministries, and families. It encourages going the extra mile and staying with family members throughout their healing journey. The book's impact extends globally through powerful prayers at the end of each chapter, akin to the lyrics of a song. Let these concise prayers permeate your heart, empowering your voice to release them into the atmosphere, breaking the shackles of all forms of abuse.

As I near the completion of 'This Happen to You,' my heartfelt prayer is that this book serves as a powerful tool to open the eyes of those who may be unaware. It aims to educate not only schools, teachers, and church ministries but also various agencies on effective strategies for healing the damaged emotions resulting from physical abuse, domestic challenges, and the experiences of young ladies embarking on their college journey.

As I was searching the bible for child abuse, I could not find it. However, God led me to 14. When Jesus saw this, he was indignant. He said to them, "Let the little children come to me and do not hinder them, for the kingdom of God belongs to such as these.

Mark 10:14 He is saying children hold a special place in God's heart, and anyone who harms a child is inviting God's wrath upon himself. 14When the disciples tried to keep the children from Jesus, He rebuked them and welcomed the children to his side, saying, "Let the little children come to me and do not hinder them for the Kingdom of God belongs to such as these. He took the kids into his arms. The word of

God promotes children to be blessed and not abused. If I may encourage a parent whose child has been victimized, they can be restored back to the innocence of their childhood. Jesus employs a parable of hurt and pain to encourage the cultivation of a childlike faith. What this suggests is that we are to entrust God with the healing of our children, embracing a straightforward and pure approach grounded in the Word. Our commitment extends to the well-being of our children's minds, bodies, souls, and spirits. Drawing inspiration from Ephesians 4:15, the directive is clear: communicate the truth with love, fostering growth towards the maturity embodied by Christ, who serves as the head of our collective body.

From him, the whole body, joined and held together by every supporting ligament, grows and builds itself up in love as each part does its work. Mark 10: 14-15 NIV. It's through the lyrics of a song, " Loud and Clear," from the Life Church in Memphis, TN, that the Holy Spirit calls intercessors worldwide to use their voices and gifts of prayer to come into agreement with God. My prayers are for victims to be healed in their minds, bodies, soul, and spirts of their life.

With every step we take uphill, our words echo into the atmosphere, contributing to the healing of hidden emotions each day. We speak safety over college campuses, within the walls of homes grappling with domestic violence, and into the atmosphere for those who harm children. Our prayers extend to the children lying in their beds, tears streaming down their faces in silence, seeking solace and restoration.

May our collective voice bring comfort, protection, and healing to those in need.

Prayer:
What About the Children?

Father, in the name of Jesus, we enter into your presence for the children of child abuse, sexual abuse, and college student that have been raped. Father, blow a fresh wind and raise up true intercessors that will go deep for this cause, allowing them to be the go-between with the Father on their behalf. O God, we need your grace to guide us to a place of healing, Giving us the faith so our children will be safe.

Father, in the name of Jesus, we humbly seek your divine intervention. Restore faith in the hearts of children and families, empowering them to reach the unreachable in their journey of healing. Let your healing touch make them whole again, filling the broken spaces with your grace and love.

Father, thank you for the faith to fight the unbeatable pain and conquer the abuses. O God, raise the children up to stand on the mountains of their life. Raise them up in the Name of Jesus.

Amen.

Pray with Power

1The Spirit of the Lord God is upon me because the Lord has anointed me to bring good news to the afflicted. He has sent me to bind up the brokenhearted, to proclaim liberty to captives and freedom to prisoners.

2To proclaim the favorable year of the Lord, and the day of vengeance of our God, to comfort all who mourn.

3To grant those who mourn in Zion, Giving them a garland instead of ashes, The oil of gladness instead of mourning, The mantle of praise instead of a spirit of fainting. So they will be called oaks of righteousness, The planting of the LORD, that He may be glorified. Isaiah 61-1-3 NAS.

In preparing to write this book and each chapter, I had to go before the throne of Grace to prepare myself mentally. I know there are many books out there from different views. This tile is so prothetic for a time like this. Looking from a different view till it happens to you or a loved one who goes through the tragedy with your healing. We look at people we know who have been through crises. We see them externally, but inside, twisted pain forms like a spider web. Abuses from the past and broken pain that has not been healed totally, and years later, you are still in darkness and still walking around full of infection, a spider web that represents emotional pain.

Looking at all the abuses, rape, child molestation, domestic violence, emotional abuse and suicidal attempt leaves people wounded with damaged emotions and psychological distress. In my twenty-plus years in ministry,

I have met many people who still carry pain. The cycle of pain persists because we often fail to address it at its root cause. Without confronting and healing the underlying issues, the affliction continues to resurface. Presently, many individuals find themselves reliant on a pill for sleep, another for waking, and yet another for balance – a desperate attempt to manage the persistent struggles. However, a higher power beckons, declaring through its word and numerous scriptures that it stands ready to provide solace. All that is required is a sincere plea for help.

It is imperative that the word of God permeates the atmosphere, bringing healing to victims of rape, safeguarding the innocence of children, and fostering a secure environment within educational institutions. The time has come to put an end to these abuses and to break free from the mental shackles that bind us. Let us empower our minds with the transformative influence of God's word.

Maybe through this book a celebrity will do a collaborative song to heal so many who have not received their healing yet. Find the scripture to heal your wound through what culture works best for you. It's time to break the cycle, according to God's word.

6In John 5:5-16, we encounter a man who had been an invalid for thirty-eight years. Jesus, upon seeing him in this prolonged condition, inquired, "Do you want to get well?" It is crucial to break the cycle of prolonged suffering and facilitate quicker healing for individuals today. Many people remain ensnared in pain due to a lack of supportive connections, whether from family, friends, or ministries that can empathetically acknowledge and address their struggles.

Celebrities, with their widespread influence, possess a unique platform to reach diverse nations and communities.

The book "This Happened to You" aims to convey the message that others can attest to your pain and that there is hope for healing. A higher power exists that can bring restoration through the process of healing. It is essential not to allow problems or hardships to dictate the trajectory of one's healing journey. While the search for solutions may be extensive, there is an "angel" assigned to assist in challenging situations. Numerous instances exist where God has healed and restored individuals who navigated through their triumphs and overcame their brokenness, subsequently becoming advocates for others.

God is distributing ashes for your beauty and by putting my pen to the paper, through my prayers, through the various artists of the lyrics to a song. The Holy Spirit helps others lean on him to do the same as the woman with the issue of blood, a touch, by renewing their heart transplant with beats that have a regular rhythm. The Holy Spirit restores the new DNA with deoxyribonucleic acid, which is the hereditary material in humans and almost all other organisms of the Fathers that are not contaminated. Through the lyrics of Kelley Clark, " piece by piece," allowing his healing bridge, blocking wall of infectious to cross over into new life.

When I was in undergrad, I had to take an elective course and chose a law course. In this class, we had to write an IRAC, which is a case's issue, rule, application, and conclusion. While bringing some closure in "This Happen to You," writing with the simplicity of the Holy Spirit. I'm using the analytical view of different forms of abuse. The issue is the forms of abuse that have been mentioned throughout the book. The R is God's word, which would be the law in normal causes, scriptures and verses through his word. The A is applying the right chapter and verse for each form of abuse for healing. And C is the conclusion of the admission of the abuse, steps to healing through the prayers piece by piece by breaking the cycle of repeated offenders.

In writing my first book, " This Happen to You," with the guidance of the Holy Spirit. I would like to thank various celebrities whose beautiful song lyrics resonated in my spirits, taking prayer requests and real-life situations to pen and paper. All songs I mention have a special connection to each chapter, helping people learn how to stand on the Promises of God through the songs and the word of God. In the closing of this last chapter, I felt like I was in the Arms of an Angel, another song written by Sarah McClachlan that guided me through scriptures and lyrics that the angel with intervention will help you to fly from the darkness in your life. You can and will be set free from fear, free of pain from your abuse, and free from the damage of emotions. God will dispatch your angel to fly away and bring comfort to your life if you believe.

Confessing with your mouth that you trust and believe in God for your healing is paramount. Equally important is the consideration of the heart, as in real life, a transplant involves taking on the emotions of the donor's heart. This analogy highlights the significance of adopting the heartbeat of God in our lives. By doing so, we not only embrace His healing power but also connect with His emotions and open ourselves to the intervention of the healing angels assigned to us.

The urgency lies in understanding the profound impact of aligning our hearts with God's. Through the power of prayer, one can invoke a bold and authoritative connection with God, touching areas that others may overlook. This prayerful approach leads to a transformative journey, ultimately presenting the results of healing to God the Father.

Prayer of Heart Transplant

Father, I pray in Jesus's name. Turn me with your Holy Spirit and keep me coming back to you, asking for your heartbeat in my transplant. It is your word that causes me to be alive. Through learning how to fast, giving up television, giving up social media so that you can heal me. Thank you, now my tears are washing away my pain and renewing me through your grace and mercy. Thank you for healing my emotions that have kept me bound for so long. And thank you, heavenly Father, for the restoration of spotlessness in my thoughts. Oh, Father, thank you for rest in the comforts of your arms. In Jesus' name, I pray. Amen.

Touch the Heart of God to move his hands of healing.

In writing this book, "I Didn't Ask For This," I was guided by the Holy Spirit. The inspiration came after witnessing Lady Gaga's impactful performance at the 2016 Oscars, where she sang "Until It Happens To You." To see victims walk across that stage representing all genders and cultures of the world that had been abused in one way or the other. I was overwhelmed and touched by the emotions of the victims who had survived. Through deep prayer and God, I delved into my prayer journals, reflecting on years of interceding for countless victims of abuse and emotional trauma.

"I Didn't Ask For This" will cause people to seek help through local centers, those still battling with the darkness in their lives, to live and not die. The message is clear: there is a tomorrow, and each day is a step toward healing, even if one didn't ask for the challenges they face.

Many people see their appearance as everything is all right, and they are crying for help. However, they are looking for someone who really believes in God and cares about the people of God. Two main factors are to listen to what is being shared, and they are observing you to see if they can trust you. Two questions: Who can I tell? Who can I trust?

With this book, I pray it reaches millions of people, whether through its title, a connection to a song, a relatable scenario, or a comforting passage from God's word.

God has a way of using our gifts through intercession or a song. God uses me through and continues to use me in prayer. Every scenario mentioned in this book is true, the names are confidential, and these prayer requests after ears are still safe with God and me.

11For I know the plans I have for you," declares the Lord, "plans to prosper you and not to harm you, plans to give you hope and a future. Jerimiah 29:11

References

Phone:901-525—2377

Child Protection Investigation / DCS

1407 Union Ave.

Hot Line: 877-237-004

Phone: 901-947-8956

TN Children Services

40S. Main, Ste.6th Floor

One Commerce Square

Memphis, TN #8103

Phone:901-348-3997

Lake Side Behavioral Health Syestem

2911 Brunswick RD.

Memphis, TN 38133

Website: www.lakesidebhs.com

Phone: 901-377-4733

Evangelist Barbara Hawthorne

Agape Child and Family

3160 Director Row

Memphis TN 38131

Website: www.agapemeanslove.org

Phone: 901-323-3600

Friends For Life

43N. Cleveland St.

Memphis, TN 38104

Website:www.fflmemphis.org

Phone: 901-272-0835

Junior Achievement of Memphis and the Mid –South

307 Madison Ave,

Memphis, TN 38103

Website:www.juniorachievement.org

Phone:901-272-0835

Family Safety Center

1750 Madison Ave. Suite 600

Memphis, TN 38104

Website: www.familysafetycenter.org

901-222-4400

Memphis, TN Women's Shelters

2649 Kirby Whitten Parkway

Memphis, TN 38133

Website: www.womenshelters.orf

Phone:901-531-1750

YWCA of Greater Memphis

3841 New Covington Pike

Memphis, TN 38128

Website: www.memphisywca.org

Phone: 901-382-2294

Juvenile Court of Memphis and Shelby County

Court Appointed Special Advocates (CASA)

616 Adams Ave.

Evangelist Barbara Hawthorne

Memphis, TN 38105

Phone: 901-222-0800

Youth Villages

714 inion Ext. Ste. 400

Memphis, TN 38112

Website: www.youthvillages.org

Phone: 901-320-6100

Memphis Child Advocacy Center

1085 Poplar Ave.

Memphis , TN 38105

Webstie: www.Memphiscac.org

Saving Lost Kids

312 north Oak Grove Rd.

Memphis, TN 38120

Website: www.savinglostkids.org

Phone: 1-800-308-0607

I Didn't Ask For This

Her faith Ministries

3396 Park Ave.

Memphis, TN 38111

Website: ww.herfaithministires.org

Phone: 901-324-3705